THOSE ANNOYING
CHRISTMAS
LETTERS

AND OTHER WRITINGS

I0649690

Garth Paltridge

WITH ILLUSTRATIONS BY

David Matthews

Published in 2020 by Connor Court Publishing Pty Ltd

Connor Court Publishing Pty Ltd
PO Box 7257
Redland Bay QLD 4165
sales@connorcourt.com
www.connorcourt.com
Phone 0497-900-685

Printed in Australia

ISBN: 9781922449221

Front cover design: Maria Giordano

Front cover picture: David Matthews

Dedicated to Kay Paltridge

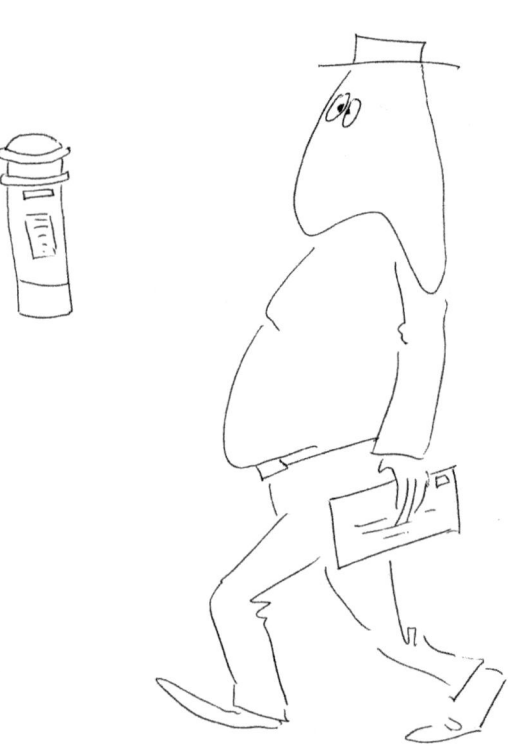

Preface

A goodly fraction of the Christmas cards my wife and I receive each year come with an attached circular letter. They make me so jealous. Invariably they tell of interesting overseas trips, of job promotions beyond the dreams of avarice, of relatives who have done marvellous things, and of great and weighty problems successfully overcome. Generally they speak of happy and interesting lifestyles beyond anything I could ever hope to lie about with any chance of success. Add to which, some of them are impossibly long and detailed.

To be fair, one has to admit that a circular letter is a handy device for dodging the writing of personal notes on each Christmas card. So nearly three decades ago we (essentially the royal 'we' here because a certain Kay Paltridge had a lot of impertinent comment to make both at the time and since) hit upon a cunning plan. We would reluctantly adopt the modern practice of composing circular letters to go with our Christmas cards, but would ensure that they contained no personal information whatsoever, or indeed anything at all of any real substance. That'd show'em! Mind you, I'm not quite sure what we thought it would show'em, but it must have seemed significant back then.

Examples of the output of the policy are presented herein. The idea of putting them together came from a number of the recipients, who no doubt believe that it is about time others could see the drivel they have had to put up with over the years, and who will get a kick out of seeing the author of the drivel making a public fool of himself.

A couple of outlier documents have been added at the end, mainly because I couldn't think of any other way of getting them into formal print other than by secreting them behind something else. Hopefully the publisher won't notice.

1993

We were brought up in that generation which was never quite sure about the propriety of circular (or even semi-circular) letters with Christmas cards. Actually we quite like getting them. Apart from their news value, they are usually typed and therefore readable. In any event Kay and I have just had our annual argument on the matter, and for this occasion have struck a compromise in the form of the following. It is, as you will see, not really a letter (circular or otherwise) but rather a use of the occasion to solve a great mystery which has plagued us for the last three years.

Back in 1966 or thereabouts Kay and I were in Wales attending some conference or other in Aberystwyth and I was struck down with a fairly impressive case of appendicitis. It was entirely Kay's fault since on the previous evening it was at her instigation that several of us went swimming in the sea at 2.00 am in the morning in waters so cold that the fish had all departed for the warmer climate of the Arctic. Funny place, Wales. In any event the aforesaid appendix was removed right there in Aberystwyth, and yours truly spent the following 10 days in hospital. Not a bad place as I remember. It served stout with the evening meal on Sundays.

Three Christmases ago I received a very nice handwritten card to the effect that the sender sorely missed me, often looked back on our previous association with love and nostalgia, hoped that we would meet again etc. etc. The usual embarrassing stuff. Kay got quite excited. The thing was postmarked Aberystwyth and was signed "Your Appendix". Suffice it to say that whoever wrote the card has been entirely successful in his or her dastardly intention. Kay and I have spent the last three years trying to figure out who it was that on the one hand knew of the appendicitis incident and on the other was visiting Aberystwyth in 1990. A parallel line of investigation has been an attempt to match the handwriting on the card with that of anyone who sends us a hand-written missive.

So awlrite – we give up! Who was it? And a merry Christmas to everyone else.

1996

You may remember that some years ago we were forced into the Christmas circular letter business in an attempt (a vain attempt as it turned out) to solve a certain mystery to do with appendices and Aberystwyth. There is no such excuse on the present occasion. It is simply laziness.

Perhaps it isn't entirely laziness. One has to face the fact that Garth's writing has of late become indecipherable even to the cognoscenti (i.e. Kay). For him actually to handwrite Christmas cards would be an exercise in futility at which even he draws the metaphorical line. So here we are. All fired up to produce deathless prose, but nothing in the way of substance on which to waste it.

Of course if one cannot mystify one can at least educate, and in that spirit it is perhaps worth relating the following wheeze which you might care to use on your next trip on a barge in central France – specifically when you are on a barge on the Canal Lateral sur Loire about five days north of your starting point. The first essential is to visit Sancerre and absorb a small quantity of the grape appropriate to the region. The second is to return to the barge and begin the southward journey back to base. The third is to blow up the engine in such a manner as to ensure valves penetrate the tops of pistons, oil flows copiously all over the engine compartment, and a degree of mechanical mayhem pertains which brings tears to the eyes of any competent diesel mechanic. In our case it certainly did to the barge owner, who was forced to transport us back via minibus to the base at Gannay – this in 90 minutes instead of five days please note – and then hand over a new and more splendiferous barge so that we could continue our journey in new pastures to the south.

All in all a good trick. One is saved the labour of retracing one's northward steps. This in turn allows one to meet up with an American couple who live permanently on a barge not far from Digoin. The husband, it seems, is once upon a time (I like the historical present tense, don't you?) a criminal lawyer in Miami. He regales one with stories of how the hoods of Miami are always turning up with suitcases full of a million dollars asking to be got off their latest murder charge. Personally we are of the opinion that he probably takes one or three too many of the aforesaid suitcases and is therefore not really in a position to return to the USA. Still, that's his business. One can imagine worse exiles.

The Muse has left us. Perhaps she will strike again in a year or two.

1997

Following an initial foray into the realms of poesy several Christmases ago (you may remember it dealt with mystery, intrigue and Aberystwyth), and subsequent now to the second of the series which appeared last year and which had something of a travel motif, one asks oneself whether a third might be too many. Well it might of course, but when has one ever been stopped by such considerations in the past?

The logical step from mystery and travel is probably sex, but authors of deathless prose have to be a bit careful of their audience at a time of year when the world is infested with merriment, goodwill and children. Besides which, Kay would probably censor the story and generally spoil the business. Inevitably therefore one is led to the occult, and specifically to the occult as it manifests itself in the region of Heathrow airport.

It turns out that there is a demon who has taken up residence in one of the hire-car joints just outside the airport fence. The fact is not generally known, presumably because his presence and effect are normally buried in the noise of all the other inconveniences which the powers-that-be have managed to instil into that particular airport. But he is real enough. Suffice it to say that thrice in the last decade hath one been thoroughly thwarted (phth! phth!) in one's search for the holy grail of the M25 which, according to rumour, and indeed according to your actual maps so thoughtfully supplied by the rental car people, lies just two minutes from the point of origin. Lies, all lies.

The use of the word 'one' in the above context is stretching the truth a bit. Kay was with me and was holding the map on each occasion, and I confess to falling into the error of blaming her rather than the demon until she convinced me (rather too forcibly

I thought at the time) of the error of my ways. Suffice it to say that on the last and fourth occasion in August of the present year, when we did by some miracle actually manage to find the M25 so as to carry out our instructions from the rental car woman to follow the signs "To the South", the demon had once again been at work. South had been obliterated from the Earth and all available signs pointed "To the West" and "To the East". And of course of those two available alternatives we managed to pick the wrong one, and believe it or not were very close to Oxford before being able to turn around and proceed on a journey originally aimed at Southampton.

So there you are. I can't quite see the point of the story now that I look back at it, but one can't have everything. Perhaps next time an application will be made to the Muse a little earlier in the process.

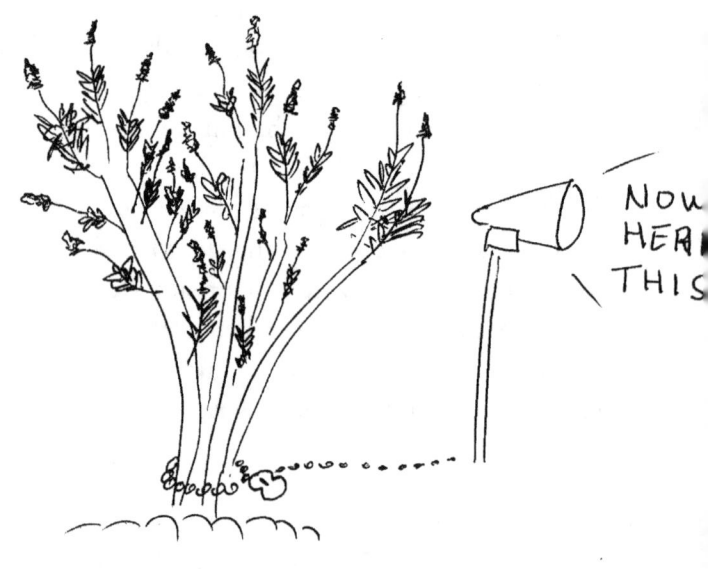

1999

The issuance of these Yuletide encyclicals has a certain religious feel to it. And to the extent that the things resemble tablets from on high then OK, I for one am not going to disabuse anyone. This particular missive proffers wise advice about the opposite sex. Namely, and to coin a phrase, that they are more deadly than the male.

Imagine the vast acreage of the Paltridge front yard. Until this year it was a veritable wasteland graced only by leaning letterbox and a few square feet of inhospitable soil. After much labour (let us not say exactly whose labour since Kay is not here to put the record straight) and considerable expense (well we know whose that was) seven large rose bushes and twelve small lavender plants were installed – this in an altruistic attempt to raise the standard of the street. And so they did. Until, that is, the rose bushes began to disappear one at a time. And until, the remaining rose bushes having been chained to the fence with massive padlocks which soon became the talk of the town, the lavender bushes in their turn began to vanish.

Acting swiftly as is one's wont, it was ensured that each and every bush was 'wired for sound'. Not your miserable ordinary asthmatic apologetic sort of sound, but something more akin to the foghorn of the Titanic. Suffice it to say that, shortly thereafter at the very moment when one was entering the shower, the foghorn gave of its best and one was forced to appear naked and yelling on the balcony which overlooks the garden, the street and (as it soon transpired) numerous pedestrians attracted by the noise. It was all a bit like a French farce, and like a French farce, took some time to sort out. The point being that it was a well-dressed and obviously well-heeled woman who, with the aplomb of the born criminal, simply disappeared into the gathering dusk bearing two of our lavender bushes. Cucumbers were not as cool as she.

Since that incident the roses themselves have been picked mercilessly by an element of the passing parade which, once again, and here I speak only of yesterday, turns out to be female. Caught in the act she was, and quite unrepentant when loudly confronted with her theft after a hundred-yard pursuit. The language was terrible. Hers I mean. And one was not really up to belting young ladies (well young women anyway) over the head with the nearest brick. She was bigger than I was. So what else is there but to complain about the business in a Christmas letter.

2000

One has the sneaking suspicion that there is more to the business of sport than simply the health of the person being pressured into it. Why, for instance, is the government so keen on promulgating the virtue of exercise when it is so obviously in its best interest not to have a population of bouncing citizens all gung-ho and capable of creating mayhem for the powers-that-be. To say nothing of the medical profession. If ever there was a biased constituency, then there it is. Just think of all the health problems that can be traced directly or indirectly to sporting injuries of one sort or another. Just think of the money that is transferred from our pockets into theirs. All very suspicious.

Now you may wonder what this has to do with the price of fish. After all, I hear you say, this letter is presumably inspired by the festive season and is one of those normal Christmas missives from the Paltridges which leave a lot to be desired by way of pith and moment. Things will perhaps be a little clearer if it is mentioned that Kay of recent times has succumbed to a dreadful disease. Not your usual, average, respectable and reasonably trivial disease associated with some unmentionable addiction, but rather, that far more severe affliction which is recorded particularly in the works of Wodehouse and certain other giants of literature concerned with the fate of mankind.

One refers of course to golf. Suffice it to say that those normal wifely duties which one has come to respect and appreciate, and on which the way of the western world has been so successfully founded, are no longer being performed. Lunch at home, for instance, has ceased to be a possibility. The chauffeured transport of the lord and master back home in the late afternoon after a hard day's work at the office has now become a random event. The dusting and cleaning of one's humble abode, previously performed, if not with cheerfulness, then at least with an eye to the good books and offices of the aforesaid l. and m., are no longer high on the list of desirable outcomes of the day.

To say nothing of the money! And this is where Christmas gets into the act. We (not the royal 'we' but that particular 'we' associated with the male half of the population) have all of us fallen into much the same trap. You know the deal. Some enormous expenditure in August on – let us say for the sake of imaginary illustration a set of ladies' golf clubs – is written off and excused on the basis of 'Oh thank you dear, lets make this my Christmas present for the year'. And of course 'we' is foolish enough to believe such nonsense and congratulate himself not only on his short-term cunning in saving at least a little from the wreckage of his account at the bank, but also more broadly on his excellent choice of life's partner in the first place. 'We' spends the rest of the year in that euphoric state of smugness normally associated with the knowledge that one has the festive season well sewn up even before the coloured lights hit the stores. Talk about living in a fool's paradise!

Shall we tell him, ladies and gentlemen? Nah! Let the idiot have a last few days of happiness before his world comes to an abrupt end on December 25th.

2001

Motor vehicles have their problems. One can be run over by them, one can run into things with them, one can be made sick by them and, so they tell me, one can get pregnant in them. More to the point, one's marriage can be put at risk because of them.

Picture a certain teller-of-tales casting through the used-car advertisements of the local rag on a boring Sunday afternoon. He spots his target, and within the hour is inspecting the sort of vehicle for which your average playboy of the western world would donate his eye teeth. It is red. It has tinted windows. It has mag wheels and wide low-profile tyres. It has a multiple CD player that subliminally transmits that essential 'boom-boom-boom' to all pedestrians within a radius of several hundred yards. And it goes like the clappers.

It is, furthermore, cheap. Or at least it becomes so when, with low cunning and not a little dastardly negotiation, he manages to lower the price by thirty percent. In short, he has both the perfect buy and proof of his mercantile skill in the one unbeatable package.

The wife in the story doesn't say all that much when the machine appears, but simply goes off in the thing together with golf clubs and associated paraphernalia to pursue her usual weekday activity. (There is a nuance here in case you aren't paying attention). She says even less as the week progresses, and it slowly begins to dawn on the hapless husband that all is not as it might be. He finally gathers among other things that she doesn't like gears. A minor sample of the 'other things' includes the machine's shape, size, colour, character and overall behaviour. The net result at the end of week – particularly as he has not been quick enough to get rid of the old car still sitting in the drive – is that he is obliged to sell the new machine instead.

Even in that mechanical process it turns out that the gods are fully against him. It rains as if there is no tomorrow on the day the car is advertised, and he bets happily to himself that no idiot will venture forth to buy a used car in weather such as this. Wrong!! And of course it takes only the one such idiot to realise the value in the deal. Admittedly the teller-of-the-tale sells the thing for two grand more than he paid, but what, one hears you cry, is a measly two grand compared with the re-capture of youth and the joy of a (nearly) new car? No doubt you can only too easily imagine the sound of falling prestige and of the descent within the home to the level of a fifth-rate power.

So we'll have none of this business of Christmas cheer thank you very much.

2002

All of you no doubt are experts on the subject of concreting around stumps in awkward spots beneath the house. The process needs skill and concentration as well as various material goods such as sand, gravel and water, together with – and it is here that things get significant – a spade. This last is required to apportion into the mixer three of this, two of that and one of the other, and indeed sometimes even a smidgen of something else. As I say, skill and concentration.

Ideally also the process needs a brickie's labourer, but it became obvious quite early in the life of our family (one learns to be observant about such things) that the discipline of brickie's labouring is one in which wives as a class find it difficult to shine. Even though, as all the world knows, the duty is writ large into the marriage vows. Wives tend to wander off on tasks of their own on each and every occasion there is nothing immediate to do. The net result is an absence of help at the crucial moment, and in turn a certain amount of screaming back and forth which does little for the job at hand and absolutely nothing for the harmony of the home. Suffice it to say that, on the occasion of which we now speak, the hero of the story was labouring alone.

Well alone more-or-less, although at some stage he vaguely noticed a female in the background mumbling to herself above the noise of the concrete mixer. She must have gone away after a while, because peace seemed to descend and he could return with clear conscience to the 'three of this, two of that' routine. At least he could have so returned if he were able to find the spade. Fifteen minutes he spent looking for the blasted thing – this in a state of increasing desperation as it became ever more apparent that Alzheimer's disease must finally have got him in its grasp. Eventually he was forced to pack things away and retire to the back of the house in search of a restorative drink and a sympathetic ear from the helpmeet working in the garden.

Working, it suddenly appeared, with the spade!!

And so to the purpose of this document. For the benefit of the coronial inquiry, it seeks advice on what action others might have taken in similar circumstances. The proximity of the season of goodwill may be regarded as irrelevant.

2004

Forgetfulness, according to some, is a sign of senility. To others, and here of course we will name no names, it is a heaven-sent opportunity to grab the upper hand in the continuing battle for household control. Experimental evidence shows that it takes only one or two lapses over a period of thirty-nine years for certain people to assume that the wise counsel of certain other people can be ignored – this on the basis that they (the certain other people) are no longer of sound mind. On the basis, in fact, that senility already has those certain other people in its grip.

Until recently the battle has not been going well around our place.

There was for instance the quite trifling

incident thirty-eight years ago of the forgotten wedding anniversary. Never forgiven of course. And there were the few (quite a few actually, but who's counting) similar lapses over subsequent years. Then there were the one or two occasions when the party of the first part simply forgot to meet the party of the second part at some pre-arranged point after work. (Matters were not improved at those times by remarking something to the effect that one's mind was on higher things. Funny that!) And finally, just a few months ago, one had cause – reasonably just cause one argued cogently but uselessly after the event – to mis-interpret an invitation to dinner. Suffice it to say that the hosts were quite nice about our turning up a week early, and indeed still managed to provide a splendid meal and an enjoyable evening. But lets face it, on the home front the price of the poor memory was pretty high. One has had to produce documentary evidence for each and every social invitation ever since.

Joy, oh joy! The worm has turned at last. Only a few days ago we managed to repeat the 'arrival at dinner one week early' trick. This time it could be proved unequivocally that the fault lay entirely with the party of the second part. Not, mind you, that 'unequivocal proof' is a concept generally appreciated by wives as a class, or indeed accepted at all by the local representative of that class. And it is true that one's initial efforts to redress the balance of household dominance have not, as yet, borne the fruit they now so obviously deserve. But one lives in hope, with eyes open and ears cocked, continuously on the lookout for other lapses on which one might develop further the campaign for regained authority.

Christmas comes early some years!!

2005

Mythology has it that forty years of marriage breeds a certain prescience with regard to the thought processes of the spouse. Not so. Not in this household anyway.

"What's for lunch?" This to wife who is mucking around doing mysterious things with food of some sort, from self who is at the kitchen table wrestling with a crossword.

"Soup".

"What sort of soup?"

"Nice soup. It'll be very good for you".

One should perhaps explain that in our

establishment "it's very good for you" is subconscious code to the effect that the food under discussion will not be eaten by the party of the female part. Either it is lousy or it has been laced with strychnine. So at this point the conversation languishes a bit, thereby enabling a quiet period of contemplation as to whether certain recent physical symptoms might relate to slow poisoning of one kind or another. Since the line of thought leads nowhere terribly fruitful, after a while one returns to the crossword.

"What's a five letter word meaning some sort of tree?"

"Cauliflower".

"What do you mean 'cauliflower' you ding dong. Cauliflower has got at least eleven letters and certainly isn't a tree".

"It's cauliflower soup".

And to be fair, so it was. Oh well. Suffice it to say that nowadays around our place the answer to all questions of life, the universe and everything is "cauliflower". At least one of us knows what we are talking about.

2006

Cats. Well one cat anyway. Specifically our particular version of the breed which, from a state of 'cat-plus' a year or two back in that he tipped the scales somewhat in excess of seven kilograms, must now be regarded only as 'cat minus' because he weighs scarcely more than a miserable 5.2 kilograms.

There could be advantages to having a slimmer, svelter(?) cat. One might imagine for instance that he would eat less, thereby saving the household a not insignificant amount by way of tinned (i.e. expensive) fish. Not so. Indeed, the decrease in feline volume seems to have been inversely proportional to intake of food in a way that can only be described as sinful. More to the point, he not only eats more, but eats it more often. Breakfast, lunch, dinner and tea are as nothing to him.

So it was a case of "off to the vet we go, tra-la". And the vet, not a bad chap in some ways when animals are not involved, of course found that the said cat has some internal problem or other that necessitates the taking of a daily pill. Not your average, white, run-of-the-mill pill, but a large, biliously orange and unbelievably expensive one that in any reasonable society would be on the national health. Suffice it to say that the blasted animal is costing us around seventy bucks a month just for pills. And he doesn't even look sick! He just purrs a lot.

Now it is here that the precision of the mention of 5.2 kilograms becomes significant. On the box containing the tablets it states in small print that, were the cat to be less than five kilograms, then one could get away with feeding him only half a tablet a day and thereby, as the mathematically literate of you will readily appreciate, save $35 a month of yours-truly's hard-earned cash. Unfortunately, the cat himself seems to have read the label on the box, and for six months now has not lost a single further gram. Blighter.

One wonders if shaving off all his fur would bring him below the magical five kilograms. Removing a leg has been deemed impractical by you know who.

2008

We (the royal plural here) were off the air last Christmas, mainly because the muse was elsewhere at the time. And in any event Kay was behaving herself more-or-less, so there wasn't all that much to talk about. This year isn't greatly different except that, according to certain quarters, senility has become an issue and the fact needs to be reported pretty sharpish before it is forgotten.

Just last week for instance we (the royal plural again) were making a gourmet lunch for ourselves. Oh how the mighty are fallen now that we have become a grass widower to golf!! But setting that aside, and thinking ahead as is our wont, a clean plate and BBQ sauce were placed upon the table while frozen chicken nuggets (a special from Coles at $3.50 if you are interested) were heating in the oven. A slight interval can be imagined during which we were passing time playing a merry tune on the piano. Well, sort of merry. And we have to admit to a certain stretching of the truth about the tune business. Whatever, the oven did its thing and went 'beep', and on the way to enquire about its problem, we found that the aforesaid plate and BBQ sauce had been stolen. An extensive search had to be instituted. Eventually the items were found in the freezer compartment of the refrigerator.

Now of course an incident like this is readily explainable in any number of quite reasonable ways. Unfortunately, none of them went down too well in a certain quarter when the tale was told on its return – the quarter's return that is. We have had to put up with strange and knowing looks about every ten minutes since then. A bit rich, you will agree, from someone who, not so long ago, parked her car in town and put the parking money in a machine on the opposite side of the road. No reasonable explanations were offered on that particular occasion. Indeed, it seems that on her return to the car, a parking attendant was at that very moment issuing it a ticket. The certain quarter was not manly enough (womanly enough?) to remonstrate with the bloke and give him the story. Rather, she made an immediate about-turn and came back later. Perhaps wisely, come to think of it. Hobart is a small town and good yarns spread fast.

Did somebody mention Christmas?

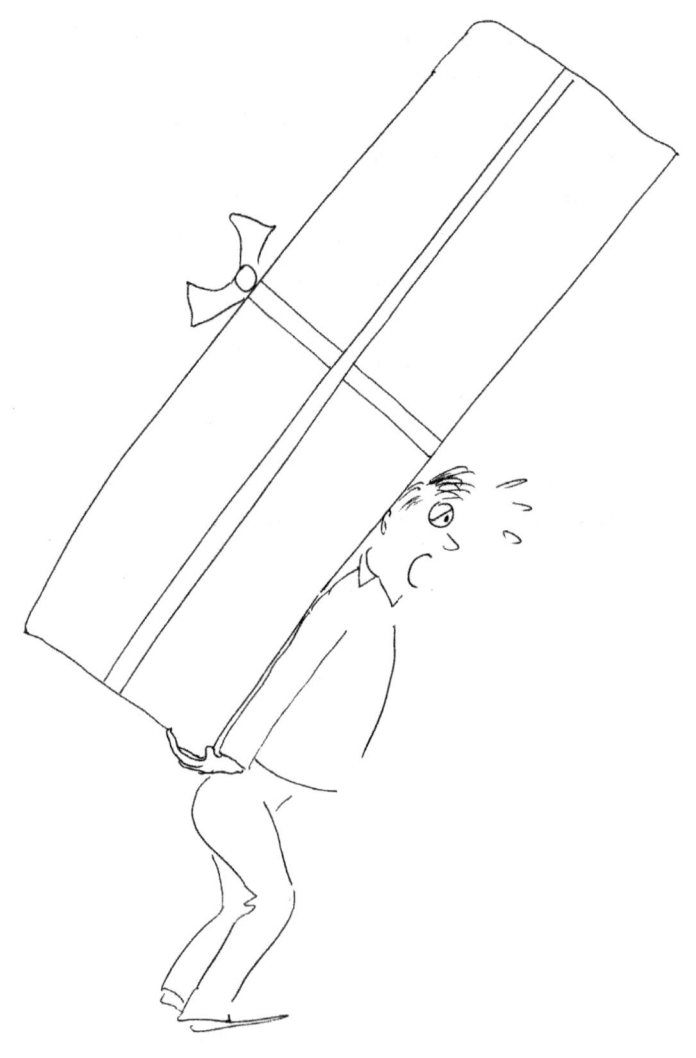

2009

Christmas brings a number of problems, not the least of which has to do with the selection of a suitable present for one's spouse. In our household, and indeed, one suspects, in most households, the main difficulty is the need to acquire something of roughly the same monetary value as whatever is the thingummy one is likely to get in return.

One is reminded of an occasion a few years back when it so happened that both Kay and I needed new wallets, and it was openly agreed between us that a Christmas gift of a wallet from each to each would be the go. Unfortunately this blatant violation of the etiquette of exchanging presents led in turn to a further suggestion that perhaps we should salt our gifts with a fifty-dollar note. The trouble was, of course, that neither of us could trust the other to keep their word. Suffice it to say that the whole idea of wallets went by the board, and we were forced back to the old ploy of giving socks and handkerchiefs. Not, mind you, that I have any particular objection to socks and handkerchiefs. In fact I quite like them. They are pretty cheap after all.

This year we are engaging in a slight variant of the wallet theme – namely, to acquire a pre-agreed single item for the household which is of use to both of us. Specifically in this instance, a new lounge suite. The obvious downsides to the procedure are that a lounge suite is difficult to wrap, and it costs a fair bit more than a sock. The less obvious downsides will no doubt emerge as time goes on.

Changing the subject a bit, one can report that we've got these two cats. Their baptismal names are Archie and Baldrick, but it quite often happens in times of sudden need that we can't immediately remember which name goes with which. As a consequence we have been forced to the use of "ginger bugger" and "black bugger" respectively. They were acquired at vast expense from the local cat pound, which must have seen us coming a mile off and introduced us to the things when they were kittens, which is an unfair tactic if ever I saw one. More to the point, guess who will get the lion's share of Christmas presents this year!

2011

Maintenance of one's position as titular head of a household requires considerable effort and a fair amount of cunning. One's authority can be so easily eroded by some small slip which, after a bit of not-so-innocent distortion by the party of the second part, can be perceived by that party as an indication of senility and therefore of a need to reverse the natural order of control.

A case in point.

Some little time ago it became necessary to visit the local dentist. The appointment was for 2 o'clock. Now it so happens that I am one of those thoughtful people who always leave home early for an appointment – this in case there should be a hold-up on the way. And indeed, as a consequence of this policy, on the day in question I arrived about 20 minutes early and parked just outside the dentist's rooms. I could see him through his window. It was cold outside but was warm and cosy inside the car, and quite sensibly I decided to wait a few minutes while listening to the radio before actually clocking in to the receptionist.

And of course I fell asleep. As one does in such circumstances. Suffice it to say that I was a quarter-of-an-hour late for the appointment, within which short period the dentist and his retinue had been phoning all and sundry with the news that their prize patient had gone missing. All and sundry of course included the aforementioned party of the second part, so there was no chance of keeping schtum about the business. I have to say that the said dentist and his retinue were amused with my excuse, and made a number of smart-Alec comments about the matter. Eventually I managed to get in to see him officially – this perhaps because of my whinge to the effect that it was all his fault for not regularly keeping a lookout through his window for patients who might be asleep out there.

But the damage on the home front had been done. As Bertie Wooster would have it, the stocks of Paltridge Inc. were down amongst the wines and spirits. I had sunk in fact to the level of a fifth-rate power. Since then I have had to scrape, scrabble and scrooge (rather like Mole in the Wind in the Willows?) back towards that position of respect appropriate to a lord and master.

Merry Christmas to those of you who can sympathise with the circumstances. Christmas to the rest of you!

2012

aterial for a normal Christmas missive is a bit short this year since Kay seems not to have done much that is outrageous, and yours truly has managed to keep his head below the parapet. So there is opportunity instead to provide one or two significant illustrations of how both the human and the animal worlds are out to get me. Not that I'm paranoiac of course.

Perhaps you have noticed that most people have bottles of shampoo and conditioner in the family shower recess. They (the bottles that is) are usually identified by a vaguely French name written on them in large print. Unfortunately the identification never extends to an up-front declaration of which bottle is shampoo and which is conditioner — not anyway in a script which is large enough to be read by someone in the habit of removing his spectacles before entering the shower. Why, I hear you cry, are the manufacturers creating this problem? Obviously, and quite apart from the aforesaid French connection which is no doubt a good-enough explanation on its own, the manufacturers are determined to make my life miserable.

At least some of you have cats. Have you noticed that ginger cats (the specificity with regard to colour comes about because my particular observational sample is restricted to only one cat) have a habit of catching small lizards and bringing them inside the house for inspection by their masters? Not much of a worry you might say. Wrong! The problem emerges when the aforesaid cats, unknown to their masters, use unoccupied shoes near the heater as a repository for lizards that are still alive and kicking. My shoes in particular. Cats, it seems, have no difficulty identifying the troubled and sensitive souls of this world.

Have you noticed also how a cat deposits itself slap-bang in the middle of a newspaper spread open on the breakfast table? Of course you have. And have you ever been able to dislodge such a cat for a period long enough to read any particular article through to its conclusion? Of course you haven't. Cats are after us I tell you!

One might mention finally and in passing the problem of Christmas greetings arriving in the form of circular letters. "Into each life some rain must fall" is regarded by certain insensitive people as sufficient justification for the affliction. Maybe, but why does it fall so heavily on me?

2013

Rumour has it that I am jealous of a certain lady of the house. All lies. The facts of the matter are these:

Some months ago the lady in question began complaining about her mobile phone. Identical to mine, it was one of those fiendish devices where the sending of text involved poking a particular key a certain number of times so as to insert the required letter onto the screen. The number of pokes for an individual letter was somewhere between one and four, and had to be determined with the aid of a magnifying glass. Neither of us ever bothered to send any text messages, and we were happy in our lives. Or at least one of us was. The other was doing all this complaining stuff.

As a consequence I was forced to acquire one of those smart phone disasters for the lady's birthday. The thing introduced us to a whole new world of complexity and incomprehensibility. More to the point, it created a situation whereby, should yours truly ever be asked how to do this or how to do that on the new phone, he hadn't a clue. A dangerous situation in any household, you will agree. A husband's claim to superior knowledge must be upheld on all relevant occasions or he will quickly sink to the level of a fifth-rate power.

And so, reluctantly of course, one had to go out and buy another such phone for his personal use. He could practice in secret the occult arts embodied within its machinery, and as a consequence was able to answer the manifold questions from the better half. It is a complete misinterpretation of the facts to imagine that one was jealous of the lady's new toy. Those of you who know his unselfish and generous nature will laugh at the very idea.

Unfortunately, the jealousy theory got a bit of a fillip when much the same situation developed a month or so later with respect to our cars. Kay got a new Hyundai that is fitted with lots of strange and wondrous electronic gizmos, the operation of which requires a certain quantum of insider knowledge. Once again in the spirit of unselfishness for which he is justly famous, one was forced to get an identical vehicle so as to acquire that certain quantum of knowledge – this again purely in order to be helpful. The fact that he had grown to hate his previous car (a Ford Mondeo, may its tribe decrease) is entirely irrelevant. The important thing is that jealousy didn't get into the business.

Not much anyway.

2014

This was the year when it became obvious that Someone-Up-There hates me. I always suspected it.

Our daughter in Melbourne had a birthday a few months back. Her boss, not a bad bloke in some ways, organized a gift from their group at work — specifically, a couple of tickets to the ballet. More to the point, he realized that our daughter's husband, a sensible fellow if ever there was one, wouldn't be seen dead anywhere within a hundred miles of such a thing as ballet. So he (the boss) phones Kay and asks if she (Kay) would like to go with her (our daughter) to the performance, bearing in mind that she (our daughter) would not know anything about the arrangement until the last moment. A Machiavellian scheme of this sort was of course irresistible as far as Kay was concerned, and the deal was done — this only a few days before the actual event.

The more experienced of you will twig immediately that there was no mention of who would pay the requisite short-notice airfare to Melbourne and back. Funny that. You will never guess who copped the bill in the end.

Sigh! I told you He hates me.

So you want more proof? A couple of months back, yours truly was cajoled into performing another of the many good deeds for which he is justly famous. In this particular case, it was to deliver a birthday present to a friend in a retirement home. Task done, and while backing out of the home's parking space, he was exercising extreme caution to avoid a steel fender just inches away from the near-side car door. He managed thereby to reverse slap bang into the biggest post you ever saw. Obviously the scenario had been set up with divine and exquisite judgement. Guess how much that little lot set me back!

So I don't want any presents this Christmas thank you. The cost may be too high.

2015

I may have mentioned our cat in previous Christmas correspondence. He is an extreme nuisance to all and sundry, and has by one means or another taken over the house for his own purposes. Precisely what those purposes may be is something of a mystery, but he has learnt to play the dumb, cute and defenceless animal with perfection. Mind you, he doesn't really have to work hard on the 'dumb' part of the act. He is dumb, full stop.

This year his nuisance value has turned out to be as nothing compared with the recent invasion of our property by pademelons.

"What the hell is a pademelon" I hear you cry. As well you might. For all you ignorant non-Tasmanians, it is a small scrub-wallaby known to its friends as a Thylogale billardierii — or rufous-bellied pademelon for short. Visually, it too is quite cute.

Wikipedia says they are solitary, and move into open areas after dusk to feed. Wikipedia is wrong. After dusk great tribes of them move into the open area of our concrete driveway to poo. Often and copiously. Especially on the concrete at the bottom of the front steps. Somewhere along the line they also worm their way into our fenced back garden – which, note, is far from being an open area – and proceed to eat the tops off the herbs and other stuff that Kay has laboriously planted the day before. And the day before that, and the day before that – etcetera and ad infinitum. She is more-than-a-little teed off about this. I am teed off because herbs cost money.

Expert advice on the matter has been less than helpful. It ranged from shooting the blighters (can you imagine the neighbour's reaction to that sort of caper at two in the morning — and anyway who has a gun in this day and age?) to poisoning them with

10/80 (what, with a cat around?). Kay herself devised a scheme whereby she surrounded each and every herb with inverted shashlik sticks in the form of a pointed barricade. Didn't work. Funny that. She also tried spraying the plants with garlic oil, capsicum spray and a dash of cayenne pepper. Didn't work either.

The score at this time is very definitely pademelons several, us zero. It seems likely that it will stay that way. Mind you again, the cat is happy because all the kerfuffle keeps a bit of the heat off him.

And oh yes, I nearly forgot. A merry Christmas to you all!!

OCCASIONAL ADDRESS AT A
UNIVERSITY OF TASMANIA
GRADUATION CEREMONY
APRIL 1993

Ladies and Gentlemen

The last occasion on which I was seriously involved in one of these affairs — involved that is rather more than simply sitting up here looking all academic and interested — was at my own graduation in Queensland back in the early sixties. The thing I remember most about it, in fact the only thing I remember about it, was that, at about this stage of the proceedings when an erudite gentleman was beginning his address on the answers to all the questions of life, the universe and everything, an extremely large, hairy and somewhat moth-eaten gorilla appeared on the stage behind him and proceeded to go into some unspeakable routine which quite ruined the impact of the great truths being orated from the lectern. To tell the truth the gorilla was far more entertaining and informative than the scheduled speech, and the aforesaid gentleman ultimately left the stage a broken man. All of which is simply to explain that my occasional glances to the back of the hall here have indeed some rational basis, and are not simply a nervous tic. Besides which, one of the of the great lessons in life is that one should never trust one's colleagues — particularly academic colleagues — when they are sitting behind you.

With that understood, I thought I might talk to you not about life, the universe and everything but about something equally as bad — namely depth, breadth, education in general and tertiary education in particular.

This for no great reason other than it provides an opportunity for me to ride a couple of hobby-horses in a circumstance where people cannot answer back, and also because it might go some way to making the present audience — particularly the parents in the audience — feel a little better about all the trouble to which they have been put in order for their offspring to reach this point in their lives called "graduation from the university".

You are probably aware that there is something essentially suspicious about the concept of depth in education. In fact in certain circles it can be nothing less than the kiss of death to be labelled as "an expert" — particularly if one aims at becoming a guru within the higher levels of company management or of the public service. It is a hackneyed definition that an "expert" is a person who knows a lot about very little — and an academic (the worst sort of expert) is a person who knows a lot about nothing at all. He or she cannot possibly have the breadth of vision to be trusted with the great issues of the moment.

The idea is not new. It reached its full flower with the rise of the "glorious amateur syndrome" in the great days of the British empire, and as far as I know is still alive and well in that country. The idea is certainly attractive, and has an enormous influence on our own education system and on our secondary education system in particular. There is a deliberate and well-argued move by the powers-that-be to ensure that secondary students get a taste of just about everything they are likely to run across in real life — this rather than concentrate their education on what used to be called the basic disciplines. Breadth is assumed to be more valuable than depth.

And I can make something of an argument to support the case in terms of personal experience. In all my life as a research scientist, I cannot think of any technique or concept which I have used as a professional scientist which I did not know about either in secondary school or, at the most, by the end of first year university. Accepting that contention at face value, and let us step lightly around the obvious whisper from the gallery behind me that this is why my personal scientific research is so lousy, in principle one should be able to go out as a professional scientist at the end of first year and not waste one's time with further study. More to the point, the ideally rounded citizen, to say nothing of the ideally rounded research scientist who is capable of sideways thinking and all those good things, would be someone who had spent his or her three or four years at the university doing as many first year subjects in as great a variety of disciplines as he or she could manage. It was precisely this sort of thinking which led to the development in the 60's of a vast number of "multidisciplinary" undergraduate courses at various of our new institutions of higher learning.

Attractive the idea may be, but it is largely

nonsense. If I may go back again to my own experience (and I presume that all the graduates here tonight have had much the same experience), first year was reasonably interesting, it was reasonably simple and it was more-or-less eminently passable. Second and third years were exactly the opposite. There seemed to be nothing fundamentally new, the subjects were in any event highly esoteric, complex and, in a way, repetitive both of each other and of the stuff we had heard about in first year. Most of us spent our time wishing we had done something else — medicine or basket weaving or something. And then suddenly towards the end of third year there came a sudden realization that there was after all something behind all this nonsense. That 'something' is best described as confidence. Not actually a confidence that one could pass third year, whose content was something of a blur at the time and has remained so all my life, but a confidence that "by George if I had to sit first year again it would be an absolute snap". In fact, it was a confidence (not, mind you, completely justified) that given a few weeks one could pass any first year subject in virtually any field you could name. (As an aside at this point perhaps I should mention that Max Beerbohm was heard to remark on one occasion that he had been a modest good-humoured boy and that it was the University that made him insufferable. I hasten to add that in his case the university was Oxford!)

In any event the realization was something of a quantum jump whose main immediate benefit was an ability to spot early on when addressing some problem that a particular approach would be a dead end, so that one could switch tack without wasting too much time. In other words, one could be vaguely professional about it. There are lots of analogues. The typical home handyman when he starts out changing his first tap washer will spend a vast amount of time worrying whether the house will fall down when he unscrews the label on the handle.

By the time he has renovated a house or two and become reasonably professional about it, he will have that arrogant confidence to tackle just about any fix-it job about the place whether or not he has done it before and, most importantly, whether or not it has anything to do with houses. He will tackle it with the knowledge that he probably won't make an embarrassing mess of the business, and even if he does he will be able to display that most essential characteristic of the professional and cover up the mess so no one will notice. He has reaped the value of training to a level far above that actually required in normal operating mode. He has had training in depth.

A couple of hobby-horses.

The first concerns the timing of the "awakening" at the end of third year. In those days of the 60's all examinations were at the end of the year, so that it forced us to absorb everything about everything more-or-less at the one time instead of being able

to spread the effort over several examination periods throughout the year. There are lots of arguments against an end-of year concentration, but for what it is worth it is my bet that without that concentration of effort it is much more difficult to generate the depth (as opposed to breadth) of knowledge which we are arguing here is so important. This philosophy is of course directly at variance with modern education theory, and all I can say in justification — in the true unbiased and well researched scientific tradition — is "pooh to the theory of education".

The second concerns another seductive proposition. Namely, that people in general, and school children in particular, must understand something before they can learn it. This is patent nonsense. One cannot understand something in the absence of some data to work with — that is to say, of some facts relevant to that something. And assembly of those facts requires learning — hard work with the memory. Whatever the theorists may say, depth of understanding must be more or less proportional to the amount of information one has at one's fingertips — that is to say in the mind. Nobody will ever convince me that one should wait for schoolchildren to understand the concept of multiplication before they learn their times table. The chances are one would wait for ever — a proposition I can easily support by reference to my own children. And it is very difficult to do all that sideways thinking that is supposed to be so desirable if one hasn't anything to think about. Once again, "pooh to the theorists".

Enough of hobby-horses. The bottom line of this rambling tale is a proposition that, while training in breadth is desirable, such training should follow a training in depth in at least one discipline. The confidence and professionalism engendered by a real knowledge of that one discipline or activity provides a yardstick and standard which governs our approach to other activities. A population of dilettantes who know a little about everything won't advance very far. Just imagine a population consisting of nothing but Sir Humphrey Applebies.

Depth, breadth, and now a bit about time. One of Henry Kissinger's little opuses (opii?) concerns how the Presidency of the United States seems to work. From the moment a president is elected, his days are divided into 5 and 10 minute bites and he has absolutely no time at all to think about a problem. And so the bureaucracy about him is devised (in theory at least) solely to present two or three options for his immediate decision on any particular problem. The bureaucracy does the thinking and the president does the deciding — on the spot. That decision-making process must be based entirely on the philosophy and experience built up by the president before he got the job — that is when he had the time to think about life, the universe and everything. And the system works for a while, more-or-less up to the point where his memory of that philosophy and experience begins to fade (perhaps after a couple of years) and where the bureaucracy and advisors begin to feed him loaded options which give him no real choice at all. He becomes a captive of the advisors, all of whom without exception have a particular barrow to push, and things go downhill from then on in.

This is simply an extreme example of what happens to most of us on the time-scale of a lifetime. As Kissinger himself says, life "is a continual struggle to rescue an element of choice from the pressure of circumstance". School, and particularly University, gives us time to think, and with a bit of luck to develop something of a framework of knowledge for making instantaneous decisions. The rest of our working life is a sort of downhill slide where, for one reason or another, our activities become increasingly divided into shorter and shorter bites with less and less time to examine options in detail and to separate the important from the unimportant. It gets back to this matter of depth of education. It is depth rather than breadth which gives us the longer-lasting ability to make instantaneous decisions.

None of this is exactly original stuff. We got onto the subject only because, as I mentioned in the beginning, it might go some way to explaining to the parents assembled here today that despite all the difficulties — both for them and their graduating off-spring — and perhaps despite a lot of evidence to the contrary — the effort involved in obtaining a degree with some depth from a reasonable university is rarely wasted. The proposition is more-or-less independent of whether or not one actually goes into the profession for which one is trained.

It remains only to define a reasonable university. I guess a necessary but not sufficient requirement is for the knuckles of most of the academic staff to clear the floor as they walk. However for me, the most appropriate measure is the degree of absent-mindedness of its professors, and on that scale the University of Tasmania does very well indeed. I

met one of the professorial gentlemen behind me walking across the campus some time ago and stopped to talk to him of this and that, and in the end he asked me which way he had been walking when we met. So I told him. "Oh good" he said. "Then I must have had lunch!"

A GENERAL WHINGE ABOUT

POLITICAL CORRECTNESS

(back in the 90's sometime)

Some time ago I introduced an after-dinner speaker at a meeting where the ratio of males to females was umpteen to one. In an attempt to be both polite and accurate I used the standard "Lady and Gentlemen" opening salutation drummed into me in days of yore. Wrong!!! The woman in question immediately jumped to her feet and let the assembled company know in no uncertain terms what she thought of me. Should I transgress in that way again then she promised among other things to separate viscera from innards (my viscera and innards) in as painful a way as possible. I must confess to becoming confused at this point and started the introduction again with "Gentlemen and Others", which in hindsight was not all that smart. Suffice it to say that it didn't improve the situation.

I subsequently talked to a great number of women about the incident in an attempt to determine the exact nature of my crime. This without a lot of success. If you are interested in statistics, about half of them could think of no reason for the response. The others shuffled their feet a bit and said they could see that the salutation was perhaps offensive in some way but (and here is the interesting thing) they couldn't really say why. Eventually I ran across an historian who was able at least to enunciate the crime, if not to explain how it became so. Actually it was three crimes — all arising from shocking ignorance of what are apparently central tenets of modern political correctness:

The words "lady" and "ladies" have

disappeared from the allowable lexicon of common speech. Don't ask me why, but someone has decreed that this shall be so. One can only use the words in their very original context of addressing the wives of the aristocracy. Not a lot of opportunity for that these days, but there you are.

One is not allowed these days to differentiate between the sexes — or even to acknowledge the existence of the two sexes — on any formal occasion. For that matter one is not allowed to differentiate on any informal occasion either, except (presumably) the obvious one where some sort of sex recognition would seem to be essential. Again don't ask me how this curious state of affairs has come about. It just has.

Politeness itself is now not acceptable behaviour. I couldn't swallow this proposition at first, but the historian swears it is true and when one thinks about it for a while it would indeed seem that she is correct. How many of us have seen gentlemen open doors for ladies (sic) and be roundly abused instead of thanked for that act of respect? Come to think of it, how many of us have been threatened with innards removal for using an introduction of "Lady and gentlemen"?

All of which leads to the conclusion that women have devised a new weapon in the battle of the sexes. They simply change the rules of human behaviour in some arbitrary fashion while carefully ensuring that men are kept ignorant of the fact. If my statistics are correct, they don't even tell half the women. And for those of you who say "What's new about that?" the answer is that the thing is no longer that standard ploy of the individual female which has been known and sighed over by males since Adam was a boy, but is very much a conspiracy of females 'en masse'.

May their tribe decrease, say I.

ABOUT THE AUTHOR

Born in Brisbane in 1940, Garth Paltridge attended Brisbane Boys College and Queensland University, and obtained a PhD degree at the University of Melbourne in 1965. He married Kay Petty in that year, and they are now the parents of two offspring and the grandparents of three. For 23 years he worked for CSIRO on various aspects of what is now called climate science. In 1990 he moved to the University of Tasmania where among other things he was the first CEO of the Antarctic and Southern Ocean Cooperative Research Centre. He retired in 2002, still lives in Hobart, still reads P. G. Wodehouse novels, and enjoys the freedom to be publicly sceptical about the modern theories of disastrous climate change. Nothing of the above except his wife, he says, has anything to do with Christmas letters.

ABOUT THE ILLUSTRATOR

Born in 1938, David Matthews spent two wasted years at the Adelaide School of Art as a young schoolboy. His mother was told to remove him and concentrate on making him into a cartoonist – advice he took with a pinch of salt. Woeful at maths, but good at English, he was told by a vocational guidance officer to become a bank officer. Instead, David became a newspaper journalist for almost 50 years, many of them as a senior sub-editor, including chief sports sub-editor. Along the way he married, had three children, divorced, remarried and now has five grandchildren and numerous step-grandchildren. He retired in 2003 and adopted a life of indolence.

www.ingramcontent.com/pod-product-compliance
Lightning Source LLC
Chambersburg PA
CBHW061524050726
47503CB00016B/2724